This book is to be re_____d
the last date

THIS BLOOMSBURY BOOK

BELONGS TO

....

For all my friends, mates and dudes
love Sahr xx

BLOOMSBURY
CHILDREN'S
BOOKS

First published in Great Britain in 2004 by Bloomsbury Publishing Plc
38 Soho Square, London, W1D 3HB

This paperback edition first published in 2005
Text and illustrations copyright © Sarah Dyer 2004
The moral right of the author/illustrator has been asserted

ISBN 0 7475 7140 6

Printed and bound in China by South China Printing Co.

1 3 5 7 9 10 8 6 4 2

All papers used by Bloomsbury Publishing are natural, recyclable products made from wood grown in
well-managed forests. The manufacturing processes conform to the environmental regulations of the country of origin.

Clementine and Mungo

by Sarah Dyer

This is Clementine and this is Mungo,
Clementine's younger brother.

Clementine knows a lot of things,
so Mungo is always asking her questions.

One sunny day Clementine and Mungo
went outside to play with the cat.

"Clementine," asked Mungo, "how do
cats stay cool in the summer?"

"Well, Mungo, when cats get too hot they can take their coats off," Clementine told him.

leaves are green,

"And, these trees,
why is it that some

and some are red?"
asked Mungo.

"Because, when it's time, tiny painting pig-ments go around and paint all the leaves from green to red," Clementine told him.

"And, if we dig down here in the garden, what will we find?" asked Mungo.

"Why the centre of the earth of course!"
replied Clementine.

We could start now if you lik

"I've heard it's not far," she said.

They did not get far and it was getting dark. Tired and muddy, they went home and Clementine helped Mungo get his bath ready.

"Clementine, why does water come out of the tap hot?" asked Mungo.

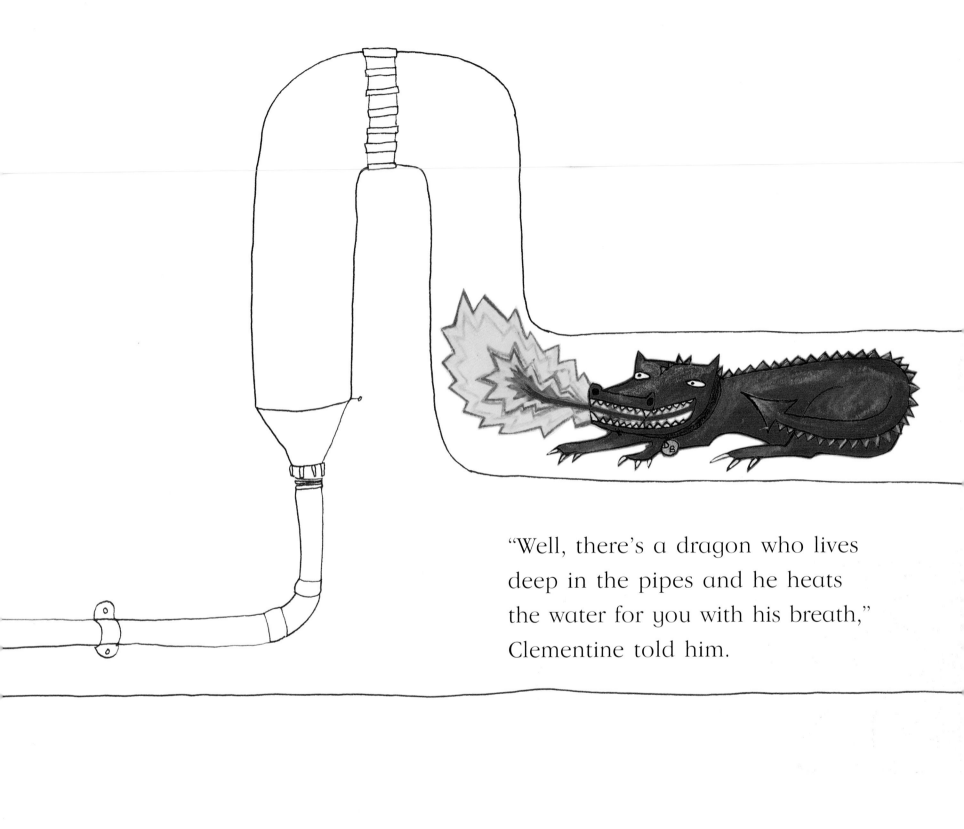

"Well, there's a dragon who lives deep in the pipes and he heats the water for you with his breath," Clementine told him.

After the nice bath Mungo was
ready for bed.
"Why do we not see the stars
in the daytime, Clementine?"
asked Mungo.

"Because, at night, a huge blanket with star-shaped holes is pulled right across the sky," Clementine told him.

After Mungo had admired the stars,
Clementine and Mungo cuddled up in bed.
Then Clementine asked Mungo a question.
"At night, when it gets very dark, why don't
you get scared, Mungo?" she whispered.

Mungo looked at Clementine, smiled, and
said, "because I know you are always there
for me, Clementine."
With that, both Clementine and Mungo
curled up together dreaming of tomorrow.

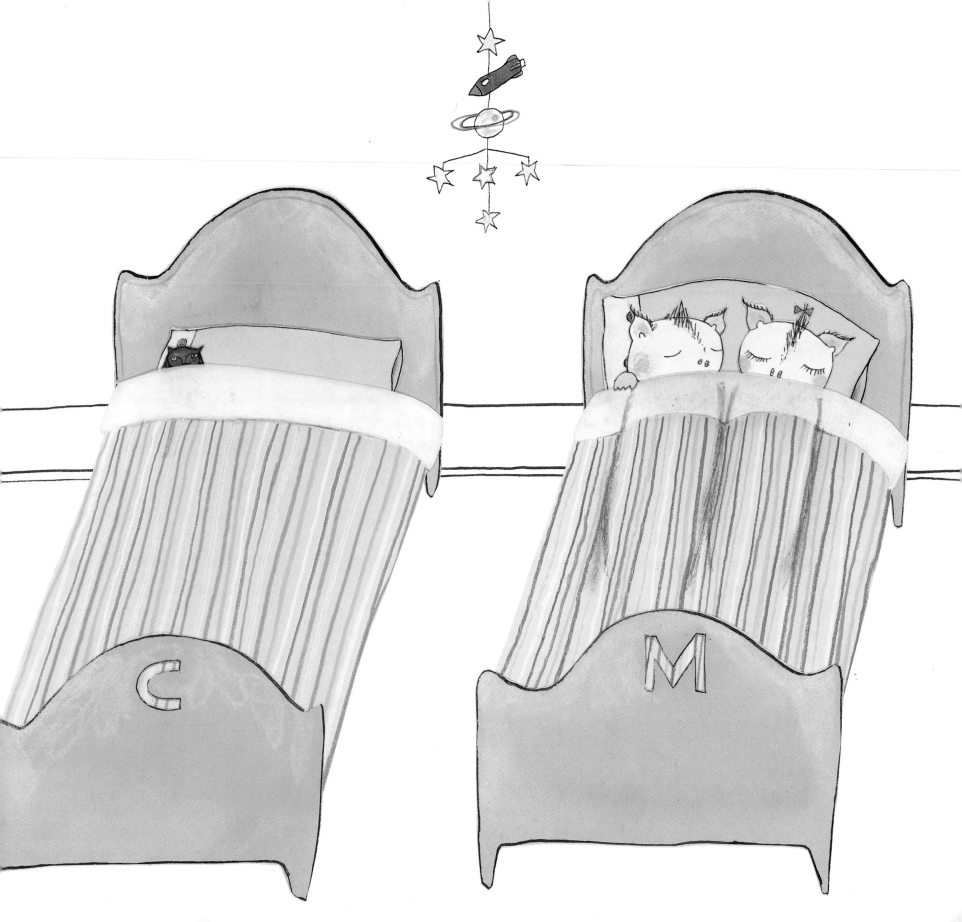

Acclaim for Smarties Prize-winning *Five Little Fiends*

'This is a truly original and wonderfully simple heart-warming picture book by a brand
new illustrator who is just bursting on to the scene'
Books For Keeps

'A simple message, boldly told, brilliantly designed – you couldn't ask for more
from a book than the stunning debut by Sarah Dyer'
Sunday Telegraph

'Important messages about sharing and the environment'
Independent

'Here's a real find: a picture book that combines eye-catching illustrations and a clever, totally original fable'
Northern Echo

'The lesson they learn in Sarah Dyer's *Five Little Fiends*, a picture book which approaches perfection,
is both seasonally apposite and timeless. It's a simple idea, which solicits tremendously complex questions'
Financial Times

'A wonderful book celebrating our world and the pleasure of sharing.
Dyer's simple text works in harmony with the pictures. The illustrations are really special'
Irish Times

'A Christmas moral for all ages'
Observer

'It is pleasing to see such careful consideration given to how the words and the illustrations
operate together in this picture book … The heavy paper and wide format ensure this beautifully
produced book is suitable for even very young children to handle'
Children's Books in Ireland

'Irresistible, thought-provoking story about the environment and sharing by an exciting new illustrator'
Financial Times

'Striking newcomer Sarah Dyer's award-winning picture book is a parable in few words …
works on several levels from literal simplicity to sophisticated metaphor'
Nicolette Jones, *Sunday Times*

'A wonderful modern tale of sharing and respect which has the resonance
and appeal of a classic picture book'
Books Magazine